TIGER WOODS

Drive to Greatness

BY
MARK STEWART

THE MILLBROOK PRESS
BROOKFIELD, CONNECTICUT

M

THE MILLBROOK PRESS

Produced by
BITTERSWEET PUBLISHING
John Sammis, President
and
TEAM STEWART, INC.

Series Design and Electronic Page Makeup by
JAFFE ENTERPRISES
Ron Jaffe

Researched and Edited by Mike Kennedy

All photos courtesy AP/ Wide World Photos, Inc. except the following:
Harry How/Allsport — Front cover
Ken Levine/Allsport — Page 18
Rusty Jarrett/Allsport — Page 29
Kansas State University — Page 6
Stamford University — Pages 26, 28
The following images are from the collection of Team Stewart:
Wilson & Co., Inc. — Page 8
Stephen Foehl — Page 16
PGA Tour — Page 20 (© 1992)
Time Inc. — Page 58 (© 2000)
Condé Nast Publications, Inc. — Page 44 (© 1997)
Golfiana — Page 51 left (© 1993)
Grand Slam Ventures — Page 51 center (© 1993)

Printed in the United States of America

Published by
The Millbrook Press, Inc.
2 Old New Milford Road
Brookfield, Connecticut 06804

www.millbrookpress.com

Library of Congress Cataloging-in-Publication Data

Stewart, Mark.
    Tiger Woods : drive to greatness / by Mark Stewart.
    p. cm.
    Includes index.
    ISBN 0-7613-1966-2 (lib. bdg.) 0-7613-1477-6 (pbk.)
    1. Woods, Tiger—Juvenile literature. 2. Golfers—United States—Juvenile literature. [1. Woods, Tiger.
2. Golfers. 3. Racially mixed people—Biography.] I. Title.

GV964.W66 S83 2001
796.352'092—dc21
    [B]   00-056624

            1 3 5 7 9 10 8 6 4 2   (lib. bdg.)
            1 3 5 7 9 10 8 6 4 2   (pbk.)

CONTENTS

FATHER OF MINE

chapter 1

> "My own background
> plays a tremendous and
> critical role in Tiger's history."
>
> *Earl Woods*

The window shattered, the woman shrieked. *It never ends,* Earl Woods thought to himself. *It never ends.* His wife, Kultida, pregnant with their first child, had been washing the dinner dishes. Luckily, she was okay. It was not the first time the neighborhood kids had pelted the Woods house with rocks or limes or whatever else was handy. Just the first time they had caused any damage. It would not be the last.

This was the "welcoming committee" in the quiet Southern California suburb of Cypress where, in 1975, Earl and Kultida purchased their first home. In a sea of white faces, a "mixed race" couple was about as welcome as a nuclear power plant. Even so, Earl Woods had known worse than this. The youngest of six children raised in Manhattan, Kansas, during the Great Depression, he faced hardship and prejudice every day of his young life.

Golf fans have gotten used to this picture. Tiger Woods
won all four of golf's major championships at a younger age than
anyone in history. According to his father, this was all part of his plan.

Earl Woods, star catcher
of the Kansas State Wildcats.

A good student and superior athlete, Earl eventually became the finest teenage catcher in the state. His mother, Maude, had a college degree, but worked as a maid because there were few jobs open to educated black women. Still, she convinced her children that education was the right path to follow. Earl remembered this lesson when he finished high school. He could have become a pro baseball player right then and there, but instead accepted an athletic scholarship to Kansas State University.

Although it had been several years since Jackie Robinson had broken the "color line" in professional baseball, Earl was the only African-American playing in the Big Seven conference. Throughout his career as a Wildcat, he was subjected to racial taunts by fans, and opponents tried to knock him down or spike him just because of the color of his skin.

After graduating, Earl turned to teaching. He had a special knack for working with kids, both in the classroom and on the athletic field. He made them proud of their successes and helped them see the positives when they failed. Earl continued to teach when he was drafted into the Army, giving lectures on military history. He also got married and had three children.

During the late 1950s and early 1960s, the military offered

> "It is heartwarming to see the lightbulb go on with some student who understands what I'm talking about. It is a light I've seen many times with my own son."
>
> *Earl Woods*

little in the way of excitement. America was "between" wars in Korea and Vietnam, so

Barrier-breaker
Jackie Robinson was
an inspiration to Earl
Woods, and later to Tiger.

officers like Earl found themselves doing boring jobs. By the mid-1960s, Earl was an information officer in Brooklyn, New York. Earl missed the rush he got from playing in a tense ball game. He felt unchallenged, and he was extremely unhappy with his life. One day, he decided to abandon everything he had come to know—including his family—and volunteered for the Green Berets.

The Green Berets were an elite, highly trained group of soldiers assigned to dangerous missions that often took them behind enemy lines. Earl was one of the oldest men in his unit, but also one of the smartest. He knew when to pull out of a tough situation and when to stand and fight. One of the men with whom he fought side-by-side was Vuong Dang Phong, a colonel in the South Vietnamese Army. He was the bravest man Earl had ever met. He and the other men had a special nickname for Phong. They called him "Tiger."

Deep down, Earl probably did not

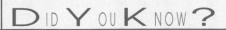

DID YOU KNOW?

Tiger Phong was captured when the U.S. pulled out of Vietnam in 1975 and died in a prison camp a year later—just eight months after Tiger Woods was born.

expect to come back from the Vietnam War alive. Some say he did not want to. He

ROY CAMPANELLA
catcher BROOKLYN DODGERS

certainly never expected to find the love of his life there, especially at the age of 42. While visiting a U.S. military installation in Bangkok, Thailand, he met Kultida, then a 23-year-old secretary.

Tida, as she likes to be called, was a mix of different races and cultures. Her father was Thai; her mother part European, part Chinese. They divorced when Tida was very young, and she spent many years away at boarding school. As she and Earl fell in love and started talking about getting married and raising a family, she made it clear that her child would never be left alone like that.

Earl survived two tours of duty as a Green Beret, and achieved the rank of lieutenant colonel. He and Tida returned to the United States as husband and wife, and in 1972 he retired from the military and took a job with a California defense contractor. In 1975, the same year Earl purchased the house in Cypress, Tida became pregnant.

Like all parents-to-be, the Woodses debated endlessly what they should name their baby. Tida invented the name "Eldrick." The E stood for Earl and the K for Kultida—it was a good name, she claimed, because their child would always be "surrounded" by his parents. Earl frowned when he heard the name. Growing up black in America would not be easy, he tried to explain; growing up with a bizarre name like Eldrick was likely to make matters worse. Earl had been in enough battles to know when he was fighting a losing one, however. On December 30, 1975, *Eldrick* Woods was born.

Almost immediately, Earl took to calling him "Tiger."

Tiger's mother, Kultida, cheers him on during a 1997 event in Thailand. Earl met Tida in Bangkok while serving with the Green Berets.

THE KID CAN PLAY

chapter 2

*"I gave him
a little putter. . .
he never let go of it."*
Earl Woods

Earl Woods had not been a very good father to his first family. But he was a great father to Tiger. He played with him, fed him, changed him, and even brought his high chair outside when he tinkered with his golf swing. Golf had become Earl's obsession after the war; he played the game whenever he could. Tiger would gurgle with delight when his father practiced his swing.

Shortly after Tiger was able to stand on his own, he wanted to swing a club, too. Earl sawed down one of his old putters and let his son try. He was amazed at what he saw: the child had a smooth, elegant swing. Earl took Tiger to the

DID YOU KNOW?

At the age of two months, Tiger could balance himself sitting on his father's hand. A few months later, Tiger was able to stand on Earl's hand.

putting green at the nearby Navy Golf Course (NGC), and soon he was knocking the ball right in the hole. A few months later, Earl took Tiger to the driving range. Every

Earl guided Tiger's career from the first day he hit a golf ball. Here he is calling
the shots in 1995 when Tiger was invited to play the prestigious Masters tournament.

time out, the boy did a little bit better. "I wasn't very strong, so I had to let the weight of the club do most of the work for me," Tiger remembers.

Tiger also remembers how he used to pester his father to go play—first on Saturdays and Sundays, but soon every day. "I learned my pop's phone number at work," he says. "I would call and ask him if I could go practice with him. He always said yes."

By the age of three, Tiger was hitting the ball out of sand traps, and even commenting on the flawed swings of other golfers! When Tiger completed the final nine holes at NGC in just 48 strokes, word began to spread that there was a golf "prodigy" in the making. A local sportscaster heard about Tiger and brought a crew out to film him for a short feature on the evening news. Producers for *The Mike Douglas Show* saw

Shots from the rough, like this one, became a Tiger Woods specialty by the age of 10.

the piece and contacted Earl. A few weeks later, Tiger was on the same program as Hollywood legends Bob Hope and Jimmy Stewart.

Naturally, Earl took tremendous pride in his son's accomplishments. But many did not. At NGC, where Earl was one of the few non-whites, some of the other members called him "Sergeant Brown" behind his back. "Brown" referred to the color of his skin; "Sergeant" was the highest military rank many white officers felt an African-American deserved. These same individuals did not like sharing the course with Earl, and it made them angry every time they saw or read something about his son.

Earl was informed by the club pro that there was a rule forbidding anyone under the age of 10 to play the course. Tiger, he was told, would have to hone his skills elsewhere. Earl responded by challenging the pro to play his four-year-old son. If Tiger won, they could stay and play; if not, they would not return. Afraid to back down from this challenge, the pro agreed to play Tiger 18 holes. Tiger would hit from the short tees, and the pro would have to spot him one stroke per hole. Tiger played magnificently, and the pro choked. Tiger won by two strokes.

The battle had been won, but the war was not over. NGC officials were furious when they heard what had happened, and overruled their own embarrassed pro. Tiger was not allowed to play. Period.

Earl and Tiger looked for other options. In the city of Long Beach, there was a par-three course called the Heartwell Park Golf Course. Most holes in golf are par-fours or par-fives, which means a player has that many shots to get the ball from the tee into the cup. A par-three course is shorter and easier, although for Tiger the greens still

> **DID YOU KNOW?**
>
> The first hint that Tiger was interested in making a difference in the world came when he was seven. After seeing a news story on the Ethiopian famine, he took a $20 bill he had been saving and asked his parents to send it to the starving children.

seemed far away. The pro at Heartwell Park, Rudy Duran, was not enthusiastic about letting Tiger play, either. He pictured a course teeming with preschoolers, and a club-house full of angry adults.

Earl asked him just to watch his son swing. It did not take long before Duran saw that Tiger was special. He not only allowed Tiger on the course, he coached him on-and-off until he was 10.

Over the next few years, Tiger continued to improve. By the age of six, he was reaching the greens that had once seemed so far away. He even made a couple of holes-in-one. Tiger was on television and in the newspapers regularly, and even started playing in tournaments. In 1982 he played in his first "international" event, the World 10-and-Under Championship, and won it.

Tiger was not the most polished golfer in his early years. His tee shots did not always go in the fairway, and he often overswung. But his concentration was fabulous, and he never lost sight of the object of the game: to put the ball in the hole. "My philosophy was to hit it as far as I could, find it, and try to score from there," he says. "As I grew stronger, I was able to control the club better and became more consistent."

BODY AND MIND

chapter 3

"I know what I want to accomplish, and I know how to get there."

Tiger Woods

Most people believe that the training of a boy or girl with an athletic gift is best left to professional coaches. They have the education and the experience to get the most out of a young star's body and mind. In golf, there are hundreds of qualified instructors. Some of the best work in the same area where Tiger Woods grew up. Yet as far as Earl and Tida were concerned, there were no better teachers than his own parents.

Tiger's mother was in charge of his "inner game." She taught her son about Buddhism, a religion that stresses how everything in the world is connected to everything else. Followers of Buddhism are encouraged to find peace by living in harmony with the world around them. To join

DID YOU KNOW?

Tiger credits his fine hand control to years of playing video games. He also says that video games helped him overcome the fear of failure. In a video game, if you mess up, it's no big deal—you just hit the reset

Tiger shows his Buddha medallion. His mother used the ideas of Buddhism to teach him how to develop discipline and inner peace.

this world without disturbing its balance, they are taught discipline, respect, and self-control. When Tida and Tiger watched sports on television together, she would point to the loud-mouthed players and warn her son never to embarrass her like that. She also told him that, if he wished to play a sport, he should play it to win. Sportsmanship was important at all times, she said, but during competition you "go for the throat," just like a real tiger, and "never let your opponent up."

Tiger took these messages out to the golf course, where Earl handled his "outer game." He made sure his son understood what each club in the bag could and could not do. He also broke down Tiger's swing and helped him analyze it. This was important, for as Tiger grew (and grew stronger) he had to make many adjustments to stay on top of his game.

Prior to Tiger's eighth birthday, Earl decided to let him in on a little secret: Golf is a game played mostly "above the shoulders." Even the most talented golfers, he

Earl and 12-year-old Tiger (far left) at a father-son tournament. Guess who won?

explained, lose their cool when things do not go perfectly. You may get an unlucky bounce, you could hear a sudden noise when you swing, or the person you are playing with might distract you. If you have the focus to block things out and maintain your concentration, Earl promised, you will never meet another person on the course who is mentally tougher than you are.

For the next couple of years, Earl put Tiger through the ultimate torture test. He would make loud noises while his son swung, he would challenge him to make impossible shots, he would roll balls in front of him while he played, and he would cheat when he knew Tiger was looking. Tiger was a very competitive child. Sometimes these

DID YOU KNOW?

As a child, Tiger dreamed of becoming the greatest golfer ever. His goal was to surpass the records set by Jack Nicklaus. Taped to the walls of his room were photos and posters of "The Golden Bear," as well as all of his career milestones.

tactics would bring him to tears. But Earl always told him that if he wanted him to stop, he would. Tiger never asked once. "He would bring me to the edge and back off," Tiger remembers.

At the same time as Earl was building his son's iron will, he was also preaching the virtues of patience. Build on everything you learn, he would tell him. Don't get frustrated if something does not come right away.

By the age of 10, Tiger was better 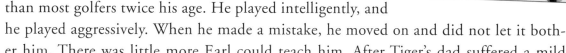 than most golfers twice his age. He played intelligently, and he played aggressively. When he made a mistake, he moved on and did not let it bother him. There was little more Earl could teach him. After Tiger's dad suffered a mild heart attack in 1986, he relinquished his coaching duties to a local pro named John Anselmo. In 1987, Tiger entered 30 weekend tournaments in Southern California and won them all.

Another important person in Tiger's training was Jay Brunza, a sports psychologist with whom Earl had become friendly. He asked Brunza to help Tiger work through the mounting pressure he felt as he entered more and more tournaments and faced increasingly better competition. At times, Brunza even caddied for Tiger so he could help him right on the course.

Technically and mechanically, there was not much improving for Tiger to do at this point. Spectators were amazed at how fast, how far, and how straight his shots flew.

14-year-old Tiger sizes up a putt. This was the last part of his game to come together.

Indeed, he coaxed every ounce of power out of his small, skinny frame. When experts watched his game, they marveled at how fast he turned his hips and how good his hands were. By twisting so quickly, Tiger generated tremendous force as his upper body swiveled through a shot. With his lightning-quick hands, he could make small, split-second corrections while he was swinging.

Once, during the final stages of an important junior tournament, Tiger took a swing that was so bad that it might have cost him a win. "Only by making a last-second correction with my hands was I able to keep the ball on the planet," he laughs. "I hit the best-looking one-iron you've ever seen. I looked over to my dad, and he was just shaking his head."

In 1991, at the age of 15, Tiger decided to enter the United States Golf Association (USGA) Junior Championship, which is open to players 18 and under. Incredibly, he won the tournament, sinking a pressure putt on the first hole of sudden death. No one his age had ever captured this prestigious event. Prior to the victory, Tiger had been viewed as a "local" phenomenon, even though he had played many tournaments outside of California (and even a few outside the U.S.). Now, clearly, he was a force to be reckoned with.

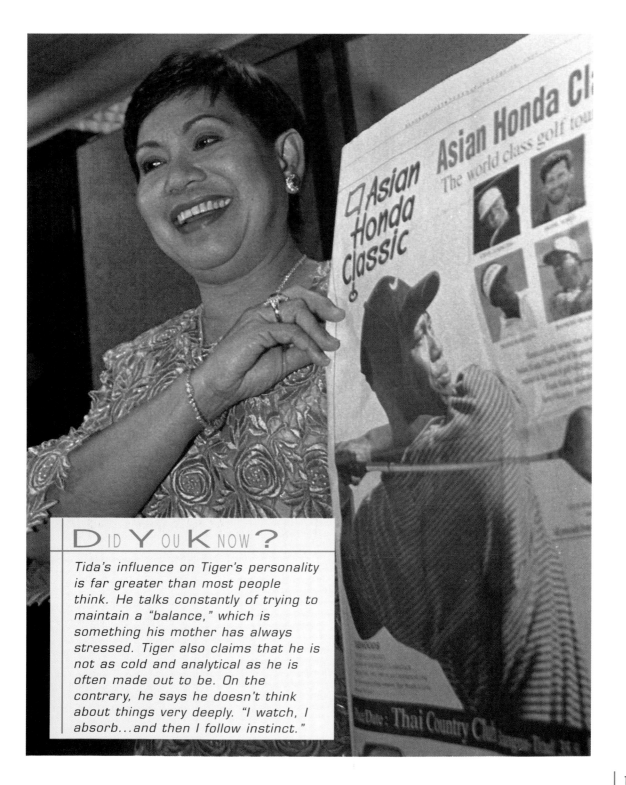

D ID Y OU K NOW ?

Tida's influence on Tiger's personality is far greater than most people think. He talks constantly of trying to maintain a "balance," which is something his mother has always stressed. Tiger also claims that he is not as cold and analytical as he is often made out to be. On the contrary, he says he doesn't think about things very deeply. "I watch, I absorb...and then I follow instinct."

JUNIOR ACHIEVEMENT

chapter 4

"The most important
thing to me is
winning tournaments.
I love winning."

Tiger Woods

One of the many people who took notice of Tiger's achievements in the early 1990s was Mark McCormack. McCormack ran International Management Group (IMG), a company that represents many of the world's top professional athletes. McCormack wanted Tiger to be an IMG client, but as long as he remained an amateur, he could not be signed. Hoping to gain an edge once Tiger decided to turn pro, IMG hired Earl Woods as a consultant. His job would be to feed the company information on promising young golfers he

DID YOU KNOW?

In 1991, the same year this card was printed, Jack Nicklaus saw Tiger for the first time. After watching the 15-year-old hit, Nicklaus said, "When I grow up, I hope my swing's as pretty as yours!"

JACK NICKLAUS

PRO SET

OFFICIAL PGA TOUR CARD

spotted while accompanying his son on the junior golf circuit.

The money was welcome in the Woods household. Earl had retired from his job several years earlier, and Tida had gone back to work full-time as a bookkeeper in order to make ends meet. Now they could afford to live comfortably, and give Tiger everything he needed to succeed. First on the list was a world-class coach. Tiger would start to grow quickly soon, but his weight was likely to remain around 130 pounds (60 kilograms). Until he filled out he would have to make some changes to his swing.

Enter Butch Harmon, the noted "swing doctor." He had worked with many of the game's all-time greats, including Greg Norman and Nick Price. Sixteen-year-old Tiger received instruction from Harmon in person, over the phone, by fax machine, and by sending videos back and forth. He made some minor adjustments, including shortening Tiger's backswing, and also designed a stretching and weight-lifting routine. When the USGA Junior Championship rolled around, Tiger won it again, on the last hole, to become the tournament's first two-time winner.

Tiger's two U.S. Junior titles earned him an invitation from the Riviera Country Club to play in the 1992 Los Angeles Open. "Open" means that a select group of amateurs are allowed to compete with the pros, even though this is a regular stop on the

A confident Tiger tees off at the 1992 Los Angeles Open. At 16
he became the youngest player ever in a PGA Tour event.

Pro Golfers Association (PGA) Tour. When it was announced that Tiger would play, it
made headlines all over the country—never before had someone so young competed in
a PGA Tour event. The news also generated several death threats against Tiger.
Although tournament officials believed these threats were the work of cowardly racists,
they were taking no chances. Tiger was assigned extra security.

A young Tiger tries to "will" a put into the hole.
His three U.S. Junior titles established a record that may never be broken.

Keeping his swing consistent while he grew was a major challenge for Tiger.

Under all of this pressure, Tiger, a 10th grader, stepped up to the par-five first tee and cut the fairway in half with a monstrous 280-yard drive. Three shots later, he holed a birdie putt. As he walked to the second hole, there was his name, atop a PGA leader board for the first time. By the end of that first day, more than 3,000 fans were following Tiger from hole to hole. And was he having a blast! Tiger was signing autographs, meeting some of the game's top players, and making shots that had tour veterans shaking their heads and smiling.

As predicted, Tiger went through a major growth spurt, which began in 1992. When it ended, in 1993, he stood 6 feet 1 (185 centimeters) and weighed about 140 pounds (64 kilograms). That year, Tiger and Butch Harmon had to make a lot of adjustments, and this caused a series of pulled muscles and backaches. He also had to change clubs a couple of times: Just when he got used to one length, they were suddenly too short.

Because of these problems, Tiger looked like a long shot to win a third national junior title—especially when he fell ill with mononucleosis prior to the tournament. But he toughed it out and advanced to the finals, where he faced Ryan Armour, a talented and streaky 16-year-old. While Tiger struggled to find his "A Game," Armour went on one of his hot streaks and built up a big lead. Tiger made some big shots and stayed close, but with two holes to play, Armour held a commanding two-stroke lead.

On the 17th hole, Tiger made a birdie to cut the deficit to one. On 18, he smashed a 300-yard drive off the tee, but his second shot on the long, par-five hole landed in a fairway sand trap. Now he had no choice but to go for the pin. This is a low-percentage shot under the best of circumstances; this was a do-or-die situation. Tiger's ball exploded out of the sand, floated toward the green, and came to a stop a dozen feet from the hole. He then rolled in the long putt for birdie. "It was the most amazing comeback," smiles Tiger. "I had to play the best two holes of my life under the toughest circumstances. And I did it."

THE TIGER FILE

TIGER'S FAVORITE...

CLOTHES: . . . . . Anything that's free— he's a legendary cheapskate.

SHOE: . . . . Nike Air Zoom, which Tiger helped design.

COLOR: . . . . Red, Tiger's "power" color.

THING TO WATCH: . . . Nature shows on television.

GOLFING BUDDY: . . . . . Junior Griffey

SPORT TO WATCH: . . . . Baseball

GUM: . . . . Dentyne

Because of his multiracial background, Tiger does not think of himself as belonging to any one ethnic group. He calls himself a "Cablanasian"— which stands for Caucasian, black, Indian, and Asian.

Meanwhile, Armour missed his birdie attempt, and had to settle for par. For the second time in three years, Tiger was in a sudden-death playoff with the junior crown on the line. One hole later, that crown belonged to Tiger. A bewildered Armour (who could blame him?) took five strokes and bogeyed the par-four, while Tiger putted out in four.

Sports fans will argue endlessly about "unbreakable" records. Many believe Wilt Chamberlain's 100-point NBA game, Joe DiMaggio's 56-game hitting streak, and Wayne Gretzky's 215-point season will stand up forever. Most golf fans think Tiger's three junior titles belong on that list, too.

Tiger follows through as a member of the Stanford University golf team.

A SPECIAL PLACE

chapter 5

*"In my own mind,
I'm always the favorite."*

Tiger Woods

Tiger turned his attention to picking a college in the summer of 1993. After considering several schools, he chose Stanford University in Northern California. Besides being one of the best colleges in the world, Stanford had a pretty good golf team. Tiger would have plenty to keep him busy there, both on and off the course. He began classes in September 1994.

Tiger loved campus life. He could be by himself, he could be the center of attention, or he could be "one of the guys." Tiger found his classes challenging, and for the first time in his life he made a group of close friends. He quickly established himself as the best player on the Stanford team, and continued to improve his game. Tiger won his first college tournament, and became the NCAA's top-ranked player in just a couple of months.

D ID Y OU K NOW ?

Before Tiger began playing for Stanford, college golf drew very few spectators. Starting in Tiger's freshman year, galleries swelled into the thousands whenever Stanford played.

The summer after his freshman year, Tiger set his sights on golf's two big amateur titles: the Western Amateur and the U.S. Amateur. These tournaments were scheduled

The Stanford golf team—one of the best ever. Tiger and his friend
Notah Begay stand side-by-side in the middle of the back row.

back-to-back, more than 1,000 miles (1,600 kilometers) apart. Tiger won the Western,
but he and his father got snarled up in Sunday traffic on their way to the airport and
missed their flight. There was just one more plane to Florida that day, and it was sold
out. If every passenger showed up and Tiger did not get on the plane, he would miss
his tee time the next day and be disqualified. Luckily, the same traffic prevented several people from making the last flight, and he and Earl made it.

This was Tiger's fourth appearance at the U.S. Amateur. He first played in that
tournament at the age of 15, and had held his own each year against older, more
experienced golfers. Now he wanted to win it. That dream almost ended in the pre-
liminaries, when Tiger found himself three strokes down with just five holes to play. In
the juniors, he could count on his opponent getting flustered. But here, he was chasing

Prior to the 1995 Masters, Tiger received a good-luck telegram from Charlie Sifford. Sifford, one of golf's first great African-American players, never got to play the tournament. He advised Tiger to ignore the hoopla and concentrate on playing good golf.

Buddy Alexander, the golf coach at the University of Florida. In yet another remarkable comeback, Tiger bore down, produced a flurry of spectacular shots, and roared past Alexander to advance.

From there, Tiger breezed to the finals, where he met Trip Kuehne. Kuehne, the star of the Oklahoma State University golf team—and a member of one of America's most famous golfing families—played magnificently, building up a five-stroke lead. With 12 holes to play, Tiger looked like he was out of it. But over the next 10 holes, he made his birdie putts and caught Kuehne.

With two holes to play, Tiger decided to go for broke. On 17 (the course's dangerous "island" green), he lofted his tee shot over the water and let the breeze carry it onto the putting surface. The crowd screamed as the ball landed near the water, then rolled to a stop about 14 feet from the hole. Tiger was pumped. He made the putt, then punched the air with his now-familiar uppercut. Tiger had won the tournament, and everyone—including a shell-shocked Kuehne—knew it. The final hole was little more than a formality. "I was in the

Tiger throws his trademark uppercut after sinking a long putt at the 1994 U.S. Amateur.

zone," Tiger says. "It's an amazing feeling to come from that many down to beat a great player."

Tiger's win qualified him to play in the Masters the following spring. The Masters is held in Georgia, at Augusta National Golf Course. The tournament's rich history and tradition make it the most prestigious event in American golf. But it also had a reputation for excluding people of color. Only three African-Americans had been invited to participate in the Masters before Tiger; it took more than 40 years before the first, Lee Elder, was allowed to play.

Tiger knew his appearance at the 1995 event would cause a stir. A young black golfer playing the Masters for the first time makes for a great story. What Tiger did not expect was how anxious the other golfers would be to meet him. One famous player after another made a point of welcoming him to Augusta and showering him with praise.

Tiger was indeed the center of attention in the early going. With Earl acting as his caddie, he shot two solid rounds of 72 and thrilled the crowd by averaging more than 300 yards per drive. After his second round, Tiger found time to give a clinic for children at a nearby public course, and also spoke with a group of African-American caddies who worked at Augusta National. They asked him if he thought a black golfer could ever win the Masters. Tiger said it definitely would happen. In fact, he personally guaranteed it.

Tiger wore his Stanford hat at the 1995 Masters.
During the tournament, he told a group of African-American caddies that a black golfer would definitely win the Masters someday.

PLAYING WITH THE BIG BOYS

chapter 6

*Against Tiger Woods,
no lead is secure."*

*Steve Scott,
1996 U.S. Amateur runner-up*

At the 1995 U.S. Amateur, Tiger was the guy everyone was gunning for, but no one even came close. There were no miracle comebacks for him this time—he dominated his opponents from start to finish. Only in the final, when he had to make up a three-shot deficit, was his second title ever in doubt. It was an important victory for Tiger. Not only did it establish him as one of the greatest amateur golfers of all time, it also taught him how to grab a lead and hold it.

Tiger also played the Scottish and British Opens in 1995. On these windswept courses, his long drives were almost useless and his medium-range play was really put to the test. Obviously, if Tiger hoped to fulfill his potential, he would need to sharpen every part of his game.

These were good lessons to learn. At the Masters, Tiger had seen that he would soon hold a unique place in his sport. Already, he was preparing to deal with all the distractions that come with playing that role.

Something else that Tiger started to sense in 1995 was how physically draining life would be as a pro. If all went well, he wanted to joint the PGA Tour sometime in 1996.

Tiger celebrates after beating George Marucci for the 1995 U.S. Amateur title. It was his second of three U.S. Amateur victories.

So when he returned to Stanford in the autumn of 1995, he hit the weight room in a big way.

Thanks to these workouts, in 1996, Tiger was bigger and stronger. On par-five "dog-legs" (where players are forced to carefully place their drives around stands of trees), he could club the ball right over the trees and reach the green in two shots. Tiger was also playing smarter. When he returned to the British Open, he picked the course apart, shooting a 66 in the second round. Finally, at the U.S. Amateur in August, he put it all together and scored a magnificent victory.

Trailing Steve Scott in the final by five strokes after 20 holes, he took his time over the final 16 and pulled even with a 35-foot putt on the second-to-last hole to force sudden death. On the second extra hole, Tiger made par and Scott bogeyed. For the third-straight year, Tiger was the country's amateur champ. "That's a feeling I'll remember for the rest of my life," he says of his long putt to tie Scott.

Tiger takes a practice cut prior to the 1996 U.S. Amateur. He turned pro after winning the tournament.

Following this tournament, Tiger announced that he was turning pro. The offers came pouring in. Everyone wanted Tiger to use their equipment, hit their ball, wear their clothes, drink their drink, drive their car, and use their credit card—and they were willing to pay him millions of dollars in return. Sensing that saying yes to too many of these offers would distract him from playing golf, Tiger only accepted a few. For the time being, at least, he limited his major endorsement deals to Nike and Titleist, a golf ball manufacturer. These deals alone gave Tiger enough money to be set for the rest of his life. That let him concentrate on playing golf and winning tournaments.

Tiger got his professional career off to a great start at the Greater Milwaukee Open. He shot an awesome 67 the first day and made a hole-in-one on the last day. The event attracted a record number of fans, most of whom spent the four days jostling for position in Tiger's gallery. Throughout the tournament, young fans hung around outside Tiger's hotel, hoping to get a glimpse of him. Each time he came to the window, they shrieked uncontrollably, as if he were a rock star.

Tiger celebrates his first professional hole-in-one at the 1996 Greater Milwaukee Open.
He finished the tournament with a score of 277, seven strokes under par.

Tiger watches a putt during the 1996 Las Vegas Invitational, the site of his first PGA victory.

Tiger's third event as a pro was the Quad City Classic. After three rounds, he looked like a sure winner. But on the final day, Tiger botched a couple of shots and took a quadruple-bogey that dropped him out of the lead, and he had to settle for fifth. At the tour's next event, the British Columbia Open, Tiger was in the hunt right to the end, but finished third.

On paper, it seemed as if Tiger was closing in on a win. In reality, he was exhausted. He chose to skip the next tournament, and canceled his appearance at a dinner where he was to be presented with the Haskins Award as the nation's top collegiate golfer for 1996. Tiger wrote more than 200 letters of apology to the dinner's disappointed guests. "I am human," he says. "I do make mistakes."

Taking a week off turned out to be a great idea. At his next event, the Las Vegas Invitational, Tiger tore up the course and came from four shots down on the final day to catch Davis Love III

DID YOU KNOW?

Tiger's magical 1996 season was marred by one terrifying event. At the Tour Championships that fall, his father suffered another heart attack. Earl's declining health meant that he would no longer be able to follow his son around the course at tournaments.

and force a playoff. One hole later, Tiger had his first PGA title. With this win, he became the hottest story in sports. At the very moment when it seemed he might cave in to the pressure of the pro tour, Tiger played miraculous golf. There was no longer any doubt that he would do great things as a professional. Now it was simply a matter of how much he could achieve and how quickly it would come.

Tiger won again a couple of weeks later, taking the Walt Disney World/Oldsmobile Classic. In seven pro tournaments, he had two victories. He was riding a streak of five top-five finishes in a row, which is something no first-year player had ever done before. What impressed PGA officials even more was the makeup of the crowd he attracted. Golf is not a sport that has been open to—or popular among—minority athletes in the United States. That also is true of the people who follow the game. They tend to be older, well-off, and white. At this tournament, there were a lot of brown faces in the crowd. And a lot of working-class people. And a lot of teenagers and kids. They were there for one reason: to cheer for Tiger Woods.

Tigger helps Tiger show off the goofy trophy
he won at the 1996 Disney Classic in Orlando, Florida.

YOUNG MASTER

chapter 7

"I'm tournament-tough this time."

*Tiger, prior to
the 1997 Masters*

If there were any doubts that Tiger Woods was for real, they were erased early on in 1997. At the Mercedes Championship, which boasts a field made up of past tournament winners, Tiger beat veteran Tom Lehman in a sudden-death playoff. At the Phoenix Open, he gave the crowd a thrill with a hole-in-one. And Tiger missed winning the Pebble Beach Pro-Am by a couple of inches. Then he and his mother jetted to Thailand for the Honda Classic, which he won by a whopping 10 strokes.

Next, Tiger set his sights on winning the Masters. He and Butch Harmon discussed the fact that the course did not favor a

DID YOU KNOW?

While in Thailand, Tiger learned that most people there consider him to be one of their own. He experienced an amazing outpouring of love, and he beamed with pride when informed that NFL broadcasts had been interrupted to show him winning the Las Vegas and Disney tournaments the year before.

Tiger admires the shot that won the 1997 Mercedes Championship.
It landed six inches from the cup.

big hitter like Tiger, so they started fine-tuning his skills from the fairway and around the green. During the three events prior to the Masters, Tiger tinkered with some new ideas and got used to the changes Harmon had suggested. No one had a hint he was "experimenting." They thought he was just in a slump. In fact, when the Masters finally began, a lot of experts claimed that Tiger's game was too inconsistent to win.

At first, it looked like the experts were right. On the first nine holes of the tournament, Tiger made four bogeys and carded an embarrassing 40. The worst score anyone had ever made on the front nine at Augusta and still managed to win the tournament was 38. According to history, Tiger had already blown it. "I was absolutely horrible," Tiger says. "I was pretty ticked off...I couldn't do anything out there."

Then something wonderful happened. "I finally decided to play some golf," he recalls.

Indeed, Tiger made one last adjustment to his swing (actually, he shortened his backswing) and began nailing shot after shot after shot. He made a long putt for a birdie on 10, chipped the ball from the fringe into the cup for another birdie on 12, then made yet another birdie on 13. On the par-five 15th hole, Tiger finished in three strokes for an eagle. He made one more birdie on the back nine, bringing his score for the day to a very respectable 70. In just over an hour, he had gone from the brink of disaster to within three shots of the lead! The next day, Tiger shot a 66 to grab the tournament lead by three strokes.

As word spread that Tiger Woods was leading the Masters, millions of people who had never watched a golf match before parked themselves in front of their televisions that Saturday to watch round three. What they saw took their breath away. Rather than folding under the incredible pressure (as so many other third-round leaders have), Tiger made the course his own. He did not hit a single bad shot, finishing with a score of 65 and a nine-stroke lead. He made golf look so easy that day, that many first-time viewers wondered what the heck was wrong with all the other guys.

An even bigger audience tuned in for Sunday's final round. There was no longer any doubt that Tiger would win the tournament. They just wanted to see if he could repeat his spectacular Saturday performance, and if he could break some records. He did not disappoint.

Tiger hits a beautiful approach from the rough on the final hole of the 1997 Masters. He won the tournament by a record 12 strokes.

Tiger and his dad hug as he walks off the 18th green after
winning the 1997 Masters. It was the proudest day of Earl's life.

When the day was done, Tiger owned the lowest score in Masters history (270) and had won by the widest margin (12 strokes). The last time someone had outshot the competition by more at a major tournament, the automobile had not yet been invented. At 21, Tiger was the youngest Masters winner, and the youngest winner of a major since 1922.

He was also the first African-American to earn the green jacket that goes with a Masters victory. On his way to the clubhouse, he spotted Lee Elder, gave him a bear hug, and thanked him for making this day possible. At the champion's dinner that evening, Tiger set another record: loudest applause. Not only were his fellow golfers cheering him, the cooks, waiters, busboys, and dishwashers came into the dining hall to clap for him, too.

Tiger, wearing the traditional winner's jacket, embraces Lee Elder.

APRIL

GQ

LOOK LIKE A PAGE OUT OF *GQ*
At Work, on the Links, Through the Night

A Better Body in 30 Days

Hot Air
Alan Deutschman on Virgin King Richard Branson

Cold Blood
Charles Bowden unmasks the world's biggest drug czar

Safe Sex
Martha Lear on how to cheat on your wife

The Coming of Tiger Woods,
Sports' Next Messiah
By Charles P. Pierce

U.S.A.: $3.00
CANADA: $3.50
FOREIGN: $4.00

04>

37122

0 757358 3

SCALING THE WALL

chapter 8

"Michael Jordan enjoyed being 'The Man.' Tiger does, too."

Butch Harmon

After the Masters, Tiger won the Byron Nelson Classic. Nelson once captured 11 events in a row—a record that even Tiger's most avid fans admit he probably will never break. After the Byron Nelson, however, the demands on the world's newest sports superstar finally began to take their toll. Between the interviews, photo shoots, commercials, and personal appearances, Tiger barely had time to draw a breath. Even when he finished a tournament far off the lead, it was Tiger to whom the media flocked. "All of a sudden I was thrust into one of the biggest spotlights there has ever been in golf," he says. "It was pretty tough at first."

Tiger did not realize it, but he was about to hit "the wall." It is an imaginary barrier that keeps even the greatest young golfers from achieving too much too soon. Golf is a game that is played largely in the mind. When the mind gets distracted by the swirl

After winning the Masters, Tiger was on the covers
of a lot of magazines—even *GQ*, a men's fashion publication.

One of the highlights of Tiger's great 1997 season was playing on the Ryder Cup team.
Veterans Tom Lehman, Jeff Maggert, and Mark O'Meara are at left;
team vice-captain Dennis Satishur is at right.

of sudden celebrity, the physical part of a golfer's game begins to suffer. That summer, Tiger found himself driving his tee shots into the rough and missing easy putts. In the season's remaining majors he finished 19th (U.S. Open), 24th (British Open), and 29th (PGA Championship). That fall, Tiger missed the cut in a tournament for just the third time since he was a teenager.

Adding to the problem was Tiger's size. For all the working out he did, he was still a skinny kid. As the season wore on, he struggled to keep his weight above 155 pounds (70 kilograms). Today he is 30 pounds heavier (14 kilograms). Tiger often lacked the stamina to do his

D ID Y OU K NOW ?

Part of Tiger's so-so second half in 1997 was the result of a paintball game he played right after the British Open. "It was fun, but I hopped over a wall and tore a few ligaments in my ankle. It was sore for about a year."

best on the final days of tournaments—days that he had once "owned." "Under the gun, on Sunday afternoons, I couldn't quite get it done," he admits.

During the weeks Tiger did not enter PGA events, he crisscrossed the country to make personal appearances, conduct clinics, appear in charity tournaments, and play pro-am events. Physically exhausted and mentally drained, Tiger barely had enough in his tank to finish the year. As a member of America's Ryder Cup team, he won just one of five matches against the European squad. Being a celebrity was a lot of fun, but it was incredibly hard work, too. "Nobody could have prepared me for the life I've had to become accustomed to," Tiger claims.

Despite all the ups and downs, 1997 was an incredible year for Tiger. His fans could hardly wait to see what he would do in 1998. As far as they were concerned, his game was perfect. And now that he had learned how to manage his hectic schedule and outside distractions, he would be able to concentrate fully on golf. Tiger looked at 1998 differently. Now that he had a grip on what was expected of him off the course, it was the perfect time to work on the flaws in his game. Toward the end of 1997, he began to make some changes.

Tiger and Butch Harmon agreed that he swung too hard. The same big swing that enabled him to smash magnificent 330-yard drives also got him into trouble when he had to hit more delicate shots from the fairway and around the greens. Sometimes the ball would go too far. Sometimes it would curve off to the side. And sometimes it would land in just the right spot, then roll far from the hole.

To shorten his mighty swing, however, would not be easy. Harmon explained to Tiger that, in the past, whenever he had changed someone's swing, other problems always arose. These problems could be fixed, but it would take time. He might go the entire year without playing four great rounds of golf in a row—and that is what it

D ID Y OU K NOW ?

Tiger became friendly with Michael Jordan in 1997, and the two talked about the demands on a young superstar as they played golf together. Jordan told Tiger that he did not have the answers he sought—each person has to cope with the craziness of fame in his own way.

In 1998, Tiger learned how to "manage" his game from friend Mark O'Meara, who won the Masters and British Open.

takes to win a tournament. Tiger told Harmon he was willing to do it. "The object of the game is to get the ball in the hole," Tiger explains. "I want to hit the ball shorter and straighter and keep it in play. To win tournaments, you have to be straight, especially since the PGA Tour has gone to higher rough and faster greens. "

As Harmon predicted, Tiger did have a tough time in 1998. He won just one event, although he consistently finished near the top of most tournaments. Tiger's fans were very disappointed. They did not realize what he was doing, and they wondered if he had lost his magic touch. A lot of people in the media who had jumped on Tiger's "bandwagon" in 1997 now claimed he was not ready for greatness.

People who knew golf, however, knew what an exceptional season Tiger was really having. To change something so basic as your swing—and to experiment and adjust while playing the pro tour—was very brave. Bravery, insists Tiger, has nothing to do with it. "The driving force in my life," he explains, "is to get my game at a level where I'll be able to compete in each tournament I tee it up."

That focus enabled him to make it through some rough times. So did the success of his friend and neighbor Mark O'Meara. O'Meara does not possess the physical gifts

One thing Tiger did not have to work on in 1998 was his concentration. After a dozen years of high-pressure golf, nothing distracts him anymore.

A more mature and focused Tiger hit the pro tour in 1999.

of a Tiger Woods. He has to "manage" his game and play within his limitations. He does not try to muscle his way around a course, and does not take chances unless he absolutely has to. In 1998, O'Meara won the Masters, then beat Tiger by a stroke at the British Open. At the end of the year, O'Meara was voted the PGA Tour's top player.

Another thing that kept Tiger focused was an observation made by Harmon. When Tiger complained about how "public" his life had become, his coach looked him in the eye and told him he had two choices. He could retire and live comfortably, quietly, and privately off the millions he had already made. Or he could find a way to enjoy life in the public eye and have fun. Tiger decided to have fun.

As the 1999 season began, Tiger's transformation was nearly complete. When he could not overwhelm a course with his body, he tried to master it with his mind. He was playing a gentler game. Tiger's tee shots were a little shorter, but a lot straighter. His irons to the green relied less on height and backspin, and more on placement and "touch." And he rarely found himself in a situation he

DID YOU KNOW?

The decision to alter his swing in 1998 was Tiger's alone. He was watching a tape of himself at the 1997 Masters and did not like what he saw. "He said his timing had been great all week," remembers Butch Harmon, "but the swing had to be fixed."

was unable to handle—on or off the golf course. "Overall, my swing, my game, my thought process is just so much better," Tiger says.

CAN YOU TOP THIS?

These are considered the all-time greatest seasons in the history of men's golf:

YEAR	PLAYER	ACHIEVEMENT
1945	Byron Nelson	18 PGA wins, including a record 11 in a row
1930	Bobby Jones	Won golf's "Grand Slam"
1953	Ben Hogan	Won Masters, U.S. & British Opens
2000	Tiger Woods	Won U.S. & British Opens and PGA Championship
1960	Arnold Palmer	8 PGA wins, including Masters & U.S. Open
1999	Tiger Woods	8 PGA wins, including PGA Championship
1972	Jack Nicklaus	7 PGA wins, including Masters & U.S. Open
1974	Johnny Miller	8 PGA wins, no majors

1937
BYRON NELSON

ARNOLD PALMER

These three cards would make up an important part of any golf collection. Byron Nelson (left), Bobby Jones (center), and Arnold Palmer (right) each enjoyed magical seasons.

NEW AND IMPROVED

"The ultimate goal is to be the best. Whether that's the best ever— who knows? I hope so."

Tiger Woods

The "new" Tiger Woods came to be during the Buick Invitational in San Diego, California. After playing two average rounds and staying in contention, he fired a 62 on Saturday and a 65 on Sunday to win the tournament. Throughout the event, Tiger struggled to find his rhythm. What made this victory so impressive was that he never really found it.

Tiger won the Buick because he stayed in the hunt on every hole, then made the really big shots when he needed them. Everyone knew Tiger could win when he was at his best. Now he

DID YOU KNOW?

After his six-straight victories in 1999-2000, Tiger had won a total of 18 PGA events in his first 76 tries, or almost 24%. During his prime years, Jack Nicklaus won just 19% of his PGA starts.

had proved that he could win when he was not. This is the mark of a great golfer. "When I didn't finish in the top ten, I was finishing 50th," he says of his pre-1999

Tiger may have shortened his backswing, but the swing itself is still a blur. The head of his club is moving at more than 200 miles (320 kilometers) per hour when it meets the ball.

game. "Now, if I'm not playing well, I'm still able to score and hang in there and give myself a chance to win. I feel I am never out of a tournament."

A great golfer must also be able to deal with the unexpected. At the PGA Championship, Tiger outdueled red-hot Mike Weir on Friday and Saturday, and thought he had the tournament won as he began the final day. But out of nowhere came young Sergio Garcia, who was suddenly playing the best golf of his life. Garcia was the man making the shots on Sunday, while Tiger's putter betrayed him on a couple of key holes. On 17, Tiger needed a stomach-wrenching eight-footer to stay ahead of the surging Spaniard. He rolled the ball right into the cup, and a few minutes later he had won his second "major."

With Tiger's "comeback" complete and Garcia playing well, there was much excitement about the possibility of a rivalry between these two young guns. Garcia hits the ball almost as far as Tiger, and is just as fearless. He also knows how to get a crowd to pull for him. Everyone agreed they would make terrific "arch enemies."

Tiger was more concerned with David Duval, another young golfer, whose skills were more polished than Garcia's. Unlike Garcia, who had yet to win a big event,

DID YOU KNOW?

Tiger is on pace to break Sam Snead's career mark of 81 victories. He needs to average just five wins a year until his late 30s and he will own the record.

If Tiger falters, David Duval is good enough to take his place at the top of the rankings. Tiger considers Duval his toughest opponent.

Duval had several impressive victories under his belt. He also had a talent for making huge shots under pressure—something that made him a threat to beat anyone at any time.

As the 1999 season unfolded, however, it became clear that Tiger might not *have* a rival. He now felt very comfortable with his new swing, and was playing round after round of error-free golf. During one awesome stretch, Tiger won eight of eleven events, including the World Cup of Golf, during which he teamed up with Mark O'Meara. There was no longer any question about it: Tiger was the finest golfer on the planet.

At the end of the year, the golf world had to catch its breath and think about how good Tiger had become. Had anyone so young ever had so much command over the game? Was there another golfer on the tour who could stand up to the pressure Tiger faced daily? Was there anyone better at holding a lead? Tiger led the PGA Tour in five of the ten major statistical categories, and he won nearly twice as much in prize money (a record-shattering $6.6 million) as the second-place player on the list.

Once again, Tiger was being compared to the all-time greats. But with his new, improved game, it was unclear whom he most resembled. Was he a young Jack Nicklaus, who got up a head of steam and simply rolled over opponents? Was he a modern-day Arnold Palmer, who fed off the excitement of a big event and drew strength from the emotion of the crowd? Or was he more like the resourceful Tom Watson, whose genius for scrambling out of trouble and making key shots earned him 34 career PGA victories? The answer is a little frightening: Tiger Woods seems to possess the winning qualities of all three!

Tiger closed out the 1999 campaign with wins in his final four PGA events. He opened up 2000 with another win, at the Mercedes Championship. Tiger won his next tournament to make it six straight! That tied all-time great Ben Hogan for history's second-longest streak.

During his amazing run, Tiger learned an important lesson—a lesson that has taken some of the sport's greatest athletes many years to realize. There is more than one way to win a golf tournament. A couple of his victories came with great final flourishes, as he scored birdies and eagles on the final few holes. But the rest came from building up a solid score over the first three rounds and playing intelligent golf on the last day. Tiger discovered that he did not have to take chances and make highlight shows to "close out" a win. He could actually put more pressure on his pursuers by playing conservative, mistake-free golf. That forced *them* to take all the chances and make all the mistakes!

Tiger's streak finally came to an end at the Buick Invitational in February. Although he failed in his bid to win seven in a row, the tournament marked a major victory for pro golf. The final round of the Buick was played on the same Sunday as the NBA

These days, when Tigers "wills" a putt into the hole, it usually goes in.

Tiger holds up the winner's trophy after his great performance at the 2000 U.S. Open.

All-Star Game, which always blows away every other sporting event on TV. On this particular Sunday, more sports fans tuned in to watch Tiger play than saw Shaq, Kobe, and Vince Carter do their thing. Golf had definitely arrived.

Tiger continued his winning ways six weeks later at the Bay Hill Invitational. Ten weeks after that, he scored an impressive victory at the prestigious Memorial. In June he entered the U.S. Open, with his sights set on winning his third major. This event is played on a different course every year, and in 2000 the site of the tournament was the treacherous course at Pebble Beach in Northern California.

Wind and rain made the play particularly tough in the early rounds. Everyone struggled just to make par, and many top players missed the cut entirely. Tiger, on the other hand, was having a great tournament. He was striking the ball beautifully, making difficult putts, and pulling off incredible saves on those rare occasions when his ball ended up in the rough. By the final day, Tiger was so far ahead of the field that the other golfers could do little more than admire how good he had become. Considering what an important tournament the U.S. Open is, and how

DID YOU KNOW?

Tiger may never dominate an event the way he did the U.S. Open. He set or tied eight U.S. Open records, and broke Tom Morris's 138-year-old mark for the largest margin of victory in a major tournament. Tiger finished 12-under-par. The second-place finishers, Ernie Els and Miguel Angel Jimenez, were each 3-over-par.

difficult the conditions were, Tiger's runaway victory must be considered one of the most awesome in the history of sports.

You the Man!

Want to know how good Tiger is? Just ask the game's top players...

"He's a boy among men... and he's showing the men how to play!"
TOM WATSON

"The rest of us will just be teeing it up for silver [second-place] medals for the next 20 years."
TOMMY TOLLES

"He motivates me to try to be better."
DAVID DUVAL

"The world has not seen anything like this kid."
ROCCO MEDIATE

"Tiger's doing something people thought couldn't be done. He's making a run at Jack Nicklaus's records."
OLIN BROWNE

"Tiger has skill and courage."
VIJAY SINGH

"He has beaten the best, time after time."
BYRON NELSON

"I'm sure he's as good as anyone has ever been."
BERNHARD LANGER

CHANGING THE GAME

chapter 10

"He's probably going to be bigger than Elvis."

Ernie Els, golf superstar

So just how good is Tiger Woods? There are many ways of answering that question. In the three years following his breakthrough win at the 1997 Masters, Tiger won 16 more PGA Tour events. During the same three years, no one else on the pro tour came close to that number. He was a better golfer in 1998 than in 1997, a better golfer in 1999 than in 1998, and a better golfer in 2000 than in 1999. To win a tournament in which Tiger is playing, a golfer must get hot, get lucky, or both. Otherwise, he can expect to watch Mr. Woods roar right by. Even when Tiger does not have his "A Game," he is a threat to win any event he enters.

SPORTS ILLUSTRATED called Tiger's U.S. Open performance the greatest ever. He thinks he can play even better!

Tiger and his friend, Joanna Jagoda, on their way to watch a tennis match.
Secure at the top of the golf world, he is learning how to relax and enjoy his fame.

A better question might be, if Tiger maintains this level of performance—or continues to improve—what does it mean for the sport of golf? So far, it has meant a lot. During those three years following the 1997 Masters, men's golf has become incredibly popular. Television ratings have soared thanks to the new fans Tiger has attracted. And prize money at tournaments has nearly doubled. As more than one pro has observed, everyone on the PGA Tour should thank Tiger every time they go to the bank.

Another part of pro golf has changed as a result of Tiger's popularity: the crowds that attend PGA events. They are bigger, louder, and many of the fans in the galleries are less interested in the tradition and etiquette of golf than in having a good time and getting a glimpse of Tiger. The PGA has always wanted to broaden its appeal, and with Tiger it has finally found a way. Now the trick is to educate new fans. Most are under the age of 25, and many have never actually played the game. "It's cool to see these people taking a serious interest in golf," says Tiger, who is happy to do his part.

Tiger works with a young golfer's grip during a golf clinic. It is one of the many ways he is bringing new players into the game.

Still another area where Tiger's influence can be seen is around the waistlines of his fellow pros. To keep up with him, a lot of players have embarked upon ambitious weight-training regimens. They know they'll have to be leaner, more muscular, and have better stamina to stay close to Tiger in the big events. Thanks to him, the PGA is seeing less beer guts and more "six packs."

Tiger's strength might also inspire some changes in the way golf courses are built. If the next generation of pro golfers puts an emphasis on raw power, par-five holes will need to have a lot more bends, breaks and obstacles. And par-fours will have to be a lot longer. When today's courses were designed, no one imagined that a player like Tiger would come along. And just because he has shortened his swing, it does not mean he has sacrificed distance. Each year since 1998, Tiger has added more muscle to his upper body, so he still can crank out 300-yard tee shots when he needs to.

The group that is most *worried* about Tiger's influence on the game might be golf writers. Pro golfers and golf writers have always had a very close relationship. Because

A hole away from history, Tiger tees off at 18 on the final day of the 2000 British Open. A few minutes later, he became the youngest player ever to win all four Grand Slam tournaments.

of some problems with the press, Tiger does not always trust that reporters will give his fans a real picture of what he is like, so he rarely grants interviews. He would rather communicate with fans through the articles he writes for *Golf Digest* and his commercials. If all of the players on the PGA Tour were to adopt this attitude, it could make life very difficult for the people who write about the game.

In the meantime, Tiger is giving them a lot to write about. In July of 2000, he played four days of dazzling golf to win the British Open. Tiger finished 19 shots under par, the first time that had ever been done in a major tournament. More impressive was the fact that, at the age of 24, he was the youngest player ever to complete golf's "Grand Slam"—winning the Masters (1997), PGA Championship (1999), U.S. Open (2000) and British Open (2000).

Tiger joined Jack Nicklaus, Ben Hogan, Gene Sarazen, and Gary Player as the only men to do this. And he did it at St. Andrews, the birthplace of golf. "To complete the slam at St. Andrews, where all golf started, makes it even more special," says Tiger.

Career *Highlights*

YEAR	EVENT	ACHIEVEMENT
1991	U.S. Junior Amateur	Becomes youngest winner at age of 15
1992	Los Angeles Open	Becomes youngest player in PGA event
1993	U.S. Junior Amateur	Wins for record third year
1994	U.S. Amateur	Becomes tournament's youngest winner
1995	U.S. Amateur	Wins event for second year in a row
1995	Masters	Best score by amateur in tournament
1996	NCAA	Wins championship
1996	U.S. Amateur	Wins title for record 3rd consecutive year
1996	Las Vegas Invitational	Scores first PGA victory in 5th pro start
1997	Masters	Wins first major by record margin
1999	PGA Championship	Wins second major with 11-under-par 277
2000	AT&T Pro-Am	Wins 6th consecutive PGA Tournament
2000	U.S. Open	Sets/ties 8 records on way to incredible 15-stroke victory
2000	British Open	Finishes a record 19-under to complete golf's Grand Slam
2000	PGA Championship	First player since 1953 to win 3 majors in the same year

A month later, Tiger captured his third major in a row, the PGA Championship. He became that tournament's first back-to-back winner since 1937, and the first player since Ben Hogan in 1953 to win three majors in the same season. Once again, Tiger finished with a record-low score. But this time he needed a three-hole playoff to seal the deal, as Bob May matched him stroke-for-stroke during the first 72 holes.

Can Tiger get a lot better? He still thinks he has a lot of room for improvement. "I don't know how much better I can get," Tiger says. "I don't know. But I can tell you one thing—I will continue to work very hard."

Tiger works hard because he loves golf and he loves to win. He encourages kids to try the game, and stick with it even if they don't do well at first. You cannot expect to be good without putting in a lot of time and effort, he explains, but the rewards for doing so can be tremendous. Winning is fun, but the *best* part of playing golf, claims Tiger, is everything you discover about yourself along the way. "Golf is a great way for someone to learn discipline, responsibility and sportsmanship," he says.

And those are things that make you a winner...both on and off the course.

INDEX